Crunchy Life

One Piece at a Time

Written By

Glen Mourning

GLEN MOURNING

DEDICATION

In a world full of challenges, children may have it the hardest when it comes to learning how to make the most out of life. And when you are fortunate enough to make it from childhood to adulthood, remember that along the way, there were plenty of grown-ups who cared for you at times, more than you cared for yourself. This book is dedicated to all of the loving adults around the world who want the most out of life for the children that they serve. It truly takes a village to get these students of ours to see their full potential.

ACKNOWLEDGMENTS

To my mother, Lillian
Without your support and unconditional love, I would have indeed given up on myself as a young man and as a student. Attending school was challenging, but when I learned how education could open the door to a better tomorrow, I learned to wake up each morning with a purpose. You made me believe in me! Thank you to all of the fantastic parents, guardians, teachers, coaches and mentors around the world. Your efforts are necessary and appreciated.

Never give up.
Success is on the other side
of your struggle.

Reading Standard question stems for developing strong independent thinkers

Why did (event) happen? How do you know? • What does (character) think about (event)? How do you know? • What do you think (character) will do differently next time? • Explain why (character or object) is important to the story.

What happened at the beginning, middle, and end of the story? • What is a summary of this story? • What is the lesson you should learn from this story? • What is this story trying to teach?

How does (character) feel at this part of the story? How do you know? • How does (character) actions change what happens in the story? • What problem does (character) have in the story? How does he/she solve their problem? • How does (character) change throughout the story? • What are (character) personality traits? How does his/ her personality affect what happens in the story? • Why is the setting important to the story?

How are the parts of the story connected? How does this section/chapter help the reader understand the setting? • How does this scene build suspense? • How would you retell this story, including important parts from the beginning, middle, and end? • In poetry what stanza is the most interesting to you? Why? • Why did the author organize the story like this? How would it be different if the order were changed?

Who is telling this story? How do you know? • Are the narrator and the author the same person? How do you know? • What point of view is this written from? • What does (character/narrator) think of (event/action)? What do you think? What would you have done differently?

Sometimes... life gets a little crunchy!

INTRODUCTION

Elite Public Charter School or EPCS, as it will often be referred to as, is a fictional charter school located in Washington, D.C. The characters and their families are based on real-life people and events.

Sometimes, life isn't as smooth or as safe as we would want it to be. Sometimes, life can get a little challenging, a little discouraging, and a little *crunchy*. Just keep on living and doing what you can to find success through all of the struggles. Just keep on chewing away. It'll always get better if you believe it will. Never give up hope.

CHAPTER ONE

Charles Anthony Thomas, aka Crunchy had become a popular student. But all of that fame didn't seem to be helping him out as a student. The fifth-grade struggle was real, and in Mr. Leroy's class, fantastic opportunities didn't make *crunchy* or challenging situations go away permanently.

All of the time and commitment that Mr. Leroy dedicated to Crunchy and his classmates, seemed to be fostering some changes. There were times when Mr. Leroy felt optimistic, but it was hard to tell for sure if his efforts were helping *all* of the students in room 227.

On occasion, Mr. Leroy told his wife that he wanted to see some major progress, but that teaching was more like planting seeds of encouragement into Crunchy and the kids. He just hoped that by the end of the year, the kids would have a solid foundation for heading into middle school.

But all in all, Mr. Leroy's effective strategies were starting to show a little. Here is Crunchy's report card from the 3rd marking period that just passed in March.

Student Name: Charles Anthony Thomas	**Grade 5 3rd Quarter Report Card**
Parent: Ms. Amani Jones	
Address: 123 Alabama Avenue Southeast, Washington, D.C	
Reading	C
Math	C
Social Studies	C
Science	C
P.E	A
Music	A
Art	A
Spanish	C

Mr. Leroy, the superstar 5th-grade teacher at Elite Public Charter School, had tried to remind his students that each and every day was a chance for them to do their best. He made it loud and clear that it was his job to care about his students more than they even cared about their own school work and well-being at times. As the warmest months of the year approached, things were seriously *heating up* in room 227.

"Okay, class…as we look forward to April, we will have to make sure to keep cool as the temperatures outside heat up," said Mr. Leroy.

Mr. Leroy had been told by teachers in the building that when the weather warms up and when state testing time gets closer, that off-task behavior spikes and student engagement drops.

"I can get the vibes that you are all getting excited for the end of the year, but trust me…we aren't there yet. We will be preparing for the big State Tests, which is why you'll have extra opportunities to practice your skills during the Easter weekend," announced Mr. Leroy.

"Man…I don't care about no dang test. All I wanna do is find the eggs with the money inside.

My grandma is famous for putting money in them eggs. It's about to be Easter," excitedly called out Kelvin. Mr. Leroy assured Kelvin that his school work would be more useful than it had been in the past.

Meanwhile at school, Crunchy spent the last few days leading up to Easter sitting in class, frustrated and confused as to why Mr. Leroy wasn't as excited as he was about everything that happened in the previous weeks. Crunchy was also upset that Mr. Leroy was assigning extra homework for all of them to do over the three day weekend.

As the week winded down the students in room 227 were getting anxious and overwhelmed. "Extra homework on Easter?" questioned Crunchy. "Why do I need extra homework? Forget Mr. Leroy and that dumb Easter bunny. I'm famous," cried out Crunchy.

During the last week of March and entering into April, Mr. Leroy had been in a better mood than he had been in previous weeks of the school year. It was as if he was preparing to celebrate something special, but Crunchy could feel that it didn't have anything to do with *him*. Maybe his birthday was coming up? Perhaps he had hit the lottery? He was already a millionaire, so maybe winning money wasn't something that would make Mr. Leroy feel the way he seemed to be feeling.

One afternoon, as the class prepared for dismissal, a smiling Mr. Leroy gave the directions for the extra assignment. The task for the students was to think of someone in their lives who had done something bad to them or to someone they loved. They then had to write that person a letter explaining that they forgive them for causing them any pain or heartache.

"And class, don't forget. Be sure to explain that whatever that person did to hurt your feelings is forgiven after they read your letter, which should mean that you no longer have any anger or grudge with them," said Mr. Leroy.

The class was dismissed, and the guys immediately began to think about who they wanted to forgive. "I'm gonna forgive my mom for making that burnt chicken last night," joked Kelvin.

"Seriously, I'm gonna write my uncle a letter and tell him that I forgive him for the time he forgot to pick me up from basketball practice. I was at the gym until the janitors packed up their cleaning supplies," added Jamal.

"Hey Crunchy, who are you going to forgive?" asked one of his classmates.

Crunchy was someone who couldn't think of the answers to questions as fast as the rest of the kids in his class. He would need a night or two or three to figure out a time when someone did something to him that he needed to forgive them for.

It was now Friday afternoon and Crunchy couldn't wait to get home and chill. When he got home he placed his bookbag on the floor near the kitchen table, grabbed a fruit cup from off of the counter and plopped on the couch in his grandma's living room. One of his older cousins had stopped by that day and had been watching a Netflix Series about Michael Jordan, the world famous basketball player. As Crunchy sat down the segment that he began watching described a tragedy that took place in 1993. Sitting there watching the show, Crunchy realized that one of his idols had lost his father to a senseless act of violence. Michael Jordan's dad was killed at the time when MJ had won his 3rd straight NBA

Championship. Crunchy couldn't believe what he was hearing and was shocked that his basketball idol was even capable of opening up and talking about such a devastating time. Crunchy began to think out loud. "Why isn't he still mad and going crazy?" As he continued watching he realized that MJ had a peace about what had happened. Somehow Jordan was able to smile, and laugh and feel like life was okay.

"If I were him…ain't no way I'd be able to talk about something that hurt so much," thought Crunchy.

The time had come for Crunchy to help his grandma clean up and get his sisters ready for dinner but the story of what happened to the Jordan family stuck in Crunchy's mind for the rest of the evening.

CHAPTER TWO

Over the Easter weekend, Mr. Leroy and his family had woken up extra early to prepare for church. Sundays were always important family days for the Leroy family. But this Sunday was special.

"Okay girls, today is Easter Sunday which means that it is especially important that we get ready and leave for church on time. Today is another day to thank God for all that he has provided us with," said Mr. Leroy.

As the Leroy family got dressed and made their way to the kitchen for breakfast, Mr. Leroy's daughters asked their dad a question.

"Daddy, why is today more special than any other Sunday?" asked Mr. Leroy's oldest daughter.

"Well every Sunday is important but today we'll be praising God with even more gratitude because Easter is the day that Jesus rose from the grave," called out Mr. Leroy to his daughters.

"Daddy, is that why you have been happier for the past couple of days?" asked Mr. Leroy's children.

"Well, I am happy that you and your sister and your mommy are so amazing and so beautiful. But yes…Easter is special because it allows us to celebrate our savior, and it is a chance for a new start. No matter what you do wrong or what someone does to you, God gave us the power to forgive people and to love everyone," answered Mr. Leroy.

Across town from the school, Crunchy and his family were preparing for a family brunch as they waited for Crunchy's mom to get home from work. Unlike Mr. Leroy's family, Crunchy and his family hadn't been to church in a while. Unfortunately for them, Crunchy's mother had to work on the weekends to earn extra money. Sometimes, she would go in to work at 4:00 a.m. and get home just before lunch time. That left Grandma Clara in charge to watch over Crunchy and his sisters.

As Crunchy's mom finished her shift, she made her way from her job back to the house. As she walked in through the front door, she saw her son trying to finish some of his work that Mr. Leroy had assigned for the Easter weekend.

"Hey, Crunchy...where is your grandma," asked Crunchy's mom as she walked into the kitchen.

"I think she's upstairs praying," said Crunchy.

Although the family hadn't been to their church in a while due to how much Crunchy's mom had to work, both Ms. Jones and Grandma Clara still believed in God.

Even after her husband was killed, Grandma Clara had never lost her faith. She had been working hard to forgive the person who took her husband's life. And on Easter Sunday, she had said a special prayer for the killer and for her husband.

"Lord, forgive your child, who took my husband's life. For he knew not what he had done, and no one deserves to suffer, not even those who harm us. Amen," prayed Crunchy's grandma.

After she was done, she came downstairs to see an upset Crunchy who sat at the kitchen table. Next to him at the table, lay three or four balled up sheets of writing paper and a ton of rubber from erasing, spread out all over the placemat.

"Hey baby, what's wrong...what do we have here?" asked Crunchy's grandma.

"Oh, this stuff. It's just a stupid writing assignment that our stupid teacher is having us do," replied Crunchy.

"Wait a minute, are you talking about the same teacher who you have been telling people was the best teacher ever?" asked Grandma Clara. "That man who played in the NFL who you were just on TV with?" questioned Crunchy's grandma.

"Well...he *was* my favorite teacher, but he don't care about me like that. All he cares about is that I figure out this stupid writing assignment," said Crunchy.

As Crunchy went on to explain what the assignment was about, his grandma couldn't help but to fight back her tears. For some reason, she had known that if Crunchy could focus and figure out who to write to, that his teacher would be doing the whole family a huge favor.

Crunchy's grandma watched and listened to him continue to struggle with not only figuring out how to start off a letter but also with figuring out who he should have addressed the letter to.

Grandma Clara decided to try one more thing. "Okay. Crunchy, baby…how about we take a break from you trying to write and just listen to one of my stories," suggested Grandma Clara.

Crunchy was always up for a story from his grandma, and he knew that every time she sat down and gave him some quality time, that afterwards, he always felt better about himself and about school.

As the two of them sat down at the kitchen table, Grandma Clara began.

"Okay, now this story is one of my favorites," said Grandma Clara.

"Once upon a time there was a little ole woman who lived in a fancy town. Every day she had to go to her job and earn money for her family so she could buy food and have clothes to wear. Her job was really far away, so she had to take the bus to get there and to get home. Each day that she rode the bus, because of the color of her skin, she was forced to sit in the back. Sometimes, if the bus was full, she would have to stand up and wouldn't be allowed to sit down at

all. She lived under the same type of rules as Ruby Bridges. So white men and women treated her really awful. One morning as she boarded the bus to get to work, there were only three seats left. Two of them were in the back of the bus where she was supposed to sit. But one of them was in the front of the bus where she was not allowed to sit. She and the other black people in town were only allowed to sit in the back. But on that day, she did not want to feel the restriction of the laws. They called these laws Jim Crow. When she thought of where to sit down, she looked at the first seat in the back. She went to sit down in that seat, but she said, "This seat is too far in the back, and it won't allow African Americans to feel like they belong and that they have the right to sit anywhere and go anyplace they choose. She passed up on sitting in that seat. The next seat she saw was also towards the back but closer to the middle. As she thought about sitting in the next seat, she said, "this seat is also far back. If I take this seat, it will remind African Americans that they can only go so far in life before they are stopped and told not to follow their dreams. This seat won't allow people of color to feel any equality. If I sit here, young African American children may not feel empowered to become lawyers, doctors, engineers, artists, professional athletes, and any other job that is hard for us to become".

So she passed up on sitting in that seat. As she made her way to the front of the bus, she spotted the last open seat. But as she looked at the spot, white men and women stared her down. As she thought about taking the seat, she felt the hatred and racism all around her. This seat was in the section where it was illegal for her to sit in. Back during this time, there were many things that black people were not allowed to do that you are allowed to do today. African Americans never sat in the section that she wanted to sit in because it was against the law. And so, being as brave as she could be, the little ole woman decided to sit in the seat towards the front of the bus. When she sat in the front, white men and women yelled and screamed at her and told her to move. A policeman even came onto the bus. When they asked her what she thought she was doing, she said, "This seat is just right, and it will help little African American girls and boys break down every barrier possible. One day all children, both Black and White will see that we are all the same and will sit alongside of one another for generations to come."

As she sat in that perfect seat, she helped change the world forever. She showed people that keeping Black and White people segregated was not going to help make the country a better place and that the only way to become united was to stand up for equal rights and better opportunities.

But on that same day, she was arrested. She was arrested and sent to jail for sitting in a seat that was only meant for white people at the time. But even after she was arrested for doing what we knew was right, it taught us that we must learn to forgive people who mistreat us. The men in her town could have surely ran up to those hateful policemen and started a fight. The people could have all turned against each other and used more hate against hate. But that wouldn't have changed anything. Instead, when people hurt you, what we should do is forgive them and show them kindness and mercy. And the same way the ole lady forgave those mean people for trying to ruin her life, I have learned to forgive people who have harmed me as well. It ain't easy to do but its better to forgive than to live your life holding grudges. So baby, just know that only love can conquer and defeat hate."

When Grandma Clara finished her story, Crunchy was absolutely sure that something like the bus situation would have upset a lot of people. Even though nobody died in the story that Grandma Clara told, Crunchy could tell by the way that she sounded when telling it that it was a very serious story and very important.

"So you gotta understand, Crunchy...we can learn to forgive anyone if we remember that God is on our side and showing forgiveness is what he would want us to do," added Grandma Clara.

Later on that day, Crunchy decided to check to see if the story that Grandma Clara had shared with him was true. As he used the family computer in the living room, he learned all about a moment in history called the Montgomery Bus Boycott. After the woman who Grandma Clara preached about was refused her seat, all of those who knew that she was mistreated in Montgomery, Alabama refused to ride those segregated buses from December 5th, 1955 until December 20th of 1955. For those two weeks, people protested and demonstrated that it was wrong to mistreat people of color regarding the use of public spaces and services.

CHAPTER THREE

The Easter Weekend flew by and time had come to head back to school. On the morning when the assignment was due, Crunchy was empty-handed. He had given the task some thought, but he couldn't figure out who in the world he needed to forgive who may have done something hurtful to him. He thought about something that one of his sisters had done, but nothing could come to his mind. He thought about something a friend or even his mom had done, and again, nothing came up.

As Mr. Leroy went through the papers that were handed in, he realized that Crunchy had not submitted a completed assignment. Mr. Leroy checked off "incomplete" into his scholar dollar tracker and then handed Crunchy a note, telling him that he would meet with him after school.

That afternoon in class, after the students were dismissed, Mr. Leroy followed up with his note and met Crunchy at his desk. Crunchy usually kept a copy of the Ebony Magazine article that featured the story of Mr. Leroy, Colin Kaepernick, and Crunchy at his seat. Although Crunchy was only mentioned in the article as a struggling student that Mr. Leroy saw potential in, he still felt a great sense of pride as his name was placed in a popular real-life magazine.

"Charles, I see that you still have your magazine copy. That was a great moment for you, but you have to find a way to create more positive memories. I'm disappointed that you didn't hand anything in for the writing task. Were you able to think of something that has hurt your feelings in the past?" asked Mr. Leroy as he chatted with Crunchy after school.

Crunchy couldn't think of anything. He couldn't come up with anything--sad. But Mr. Leroy had known one event from Crunchy's past that would be difficult to talk about, but what would be really important to discuss.

Mr. Leroy had known about the shooting that had taken Crunchy's grandad away from their family. Grandad Jones was senselessly gunned down a few years ago while walking home from work in an event which was traumatic for Crunchy. But would Crunchy open up and discuss his grandad's death? Mr. Leroy's life experiences allowed him to learn about the power of forgiveness. He had thought about helping Crunchy find comfort in the healing process of losing a loved one. Although Crunchy didn't realize it, his grandad's death was causing him more pain than he realized. Instead of jumping right into it, Mr. Leroy just tried being a friend.

"So tell me this, Charles. Who is your favorite basketball player?" asked Mr. Leroy.

Crunchy was unsure as to where Mr. Leroy was going with the question.

"Psh...MJ," whispered Crunchy.

Mr. Leroy heard Crunchy's faint response but decided to ask him a second time.

"Come on, man...who is your favorite hoop star of all time?" questioned Mr. Leroy.

This time, Crunchy was a bit more intrigued to answer the question.

"Man…MJ, Michael Jordan. Ain't nobody better than him," said Crunchy.

Standing there in class for a second, Mr. Leroy began to piece together how he could connect with Crunchy to encourage him to try his best with school.

"Why do you think he is the best?" asked Mr. Leroy.

As Crunchy stood there, a million reason as to why MJ was the greatest basketball player of all time raced through his mind. But one thing that he had recently learned about his idol stuck out the most.

"I mean…he was the best shooter, had the best dunks…won the most championships and never gave up," said Crunchy as he pointed at his fingers to signal that he had just ran off the list of reasons that solidified MJ's spot as the greatest player of all time.

"What do you mean, he never gave up?" asked Mr. Leroy. "Do you mean he never quit on the court or do you mean something else?"

Crunchy slowly tilted his head and thought about the question for a moment.

"I mean like, yeah he never quit when he played ball but like…something bad happened to him one time and he didn't quit," answered Crunchy.

The two of them stood there in the room in silence for a moment. Then, in a very quiet voice Crunchy began talking to Mr. Leroy again.

"Jordan…and his mom and the family…they lost Jordan's dad. Somebody killed him. If I was Jordan, I would have quit playing basketball, man. I heard about his life on Netflix and I would have been too sad to play ball," said Crunchy.

At that point Mr. Leroy knew that Crunchy had a ton of questions about life.

"How did it make you feel after seeing that part of the show, knowing that Jordan didn't quit and that he actually won three more NBA Championships even after his dad's death?" asked Mr. Leroy.

"Like I said, I don't know how he didn't quit after his dad died. It was almost like he worked even harder and played even harder after his dad was gone," replied Crunchy.

Mr. Leroy hesitated and then asked another question about Michael Jordan. "How do you think MJ's dad felt in Heaven when he watched his son fight through the pain to continue winning?" asked Mr. Leroy.

"Proud," said Crunchy. "Really, really Proud."

"I wonder how his dad would have felt if he gave up and quit?" asked Mr. Leroy.

Crunchy was now taking it all in. He was full of emotion and was beginning to understand exactly why MJ didn't quit. He was beginning to think about his own situation which was similar to MJ's. Crunchy began thinking about his own grandad.

"Man, this makes me think about my mom's dad…my grandad," said Crunchy.

"What about your mom's father," asked Mr. Leroy.

Crunchy took a long pause—

"Well, I mean…my grandad died a few years ago, and it's crazy that he's dead, but like, I guess that's something that still hurts my feelings," shared Crunchy.

Mr. Leroy sat for a second and didn't say much until he felt it was the right time to speak again.

"Charles, in life...we have to be able to forgive people that hurt our feelings. We have to forgive people who make fun of us, and we even have to forgive people...bad people...the same type of people who may have even sent MJ's dad and your grandad to Heaven," explained Mr. Leroy.

Crunchy took a few moments to take in all of what Mr. Leroy had said. It wasn't easy, but he began to think about every word that was spoken to him--he studied each and every word.

"My grandad was my best friend," said Crunchy.

Crunchy immediately had a flashback to his grandad, tossing him a football at the city park down the road from his grandma's house. Then, he pictured his grandad singing one of his favorite New Edition songs with Crunchy as they often pretended to be on live TV singing in the kitchen at home.

"I can't forget about him. And besides, you still have your best friend. And you and your best friend are rich and famous, so you don't even know what it's like," shouted Crunchy.

Mr. Leroy replied by telling Crunchy that he was right. Mr. Leroy's best friend Colin was still alive, and they were famous football players. But Mr. Leroy also told Crunchy that being famous and all of the money in the world can't heal your heart from hurting due to hating someone for something.

"So, my family is supposed to tell the man who killed my grandad that we forgive him?" asked Crunchy. "Why...then he'll think that it was okay to hurt people or kill people," yelled out Crunchy.

Mr. Leroy knew that it would be difficult to explain what he meant to Crunchy, but he also knew that it was important to share his feelings with him.

"Well, the other day, I heard you asking about how I was able to forgive you for misbehaving. You were also trying to figure out why I chose you to be on TV with Colin and I. I'm pretty sure that you also thought that I would give up on you. Well, Charles…the answers to those questions are simple. We forgive people because we *can*. Each day is a new beginning, and you can control what you do with your fresh start."

Mr. Leroy continued explaining, and it seemed as if a lightbulb turned on in Crunchy's head.

"We forgive because our hearts are designed to forgive people and to never judge people. Everyone deserves a chance to live their best life.

Even after someone messes up really, really, really bad, they deserve a chance to put their life back together even if they have to do it one piece at a time. And as we forgive, our own pain and anger that we have inside and that we show towards others starts to slowly fade away."

Crunchy was saddened by the thought of being asked to forgive someone who did something so awful to his family. But the thought of no longer being angered by it and no longer letting the anger control him somehow made him feel better.

Mr. Leroy went on to explain that they had just come back from a long three day weekend because of Easter Sunday. He told Crunchy that all of the mistakes that he had made during the school year were already forgiven. He went on to say that Crunchy was able to start over as a new kid each and every day.

Their conversation finished up, and Crunchy made his way downstairs to pick up his sisters. Crunchy now had a better understanding of why Mr. Leroy wasn't upset with him. He also began to realize why it had been so hard for him to know where all of his anger came from.

CHAPTER FOUR

April showers are supposed to bring May flowers. For almost every student in room 227 this school year had turned into the most fantastic school year of their lives. But for Crunchy, nothing positive seemed to last as we was now right back to his usual self, unmotivated and frustrated with his grades.

With less than a month left before the third, fourth, and fifth-graders at EPCS would have to begin the brutal two-week process of state testing, Mr. Leroy had one more unit to teach during the reading block. Even though Crunchy didn't learn exactly how to write a letter, Mr. Leroy had to move on to the last type of writing.

"Good morning, everyone," called out Mr. Leroy. "The lesson for today will be on poetry. We will have a lot of fun as long as you are all focused on what makes up a poem, and as long as you learn the new vocabulary words."

Everyone knew that poetry was for girls, but for some reason, the boys were fully alert and ready to take their poetry skills to the next level. State testing was finally approaching, but that wasn't what everyone was looking forward to.

Raising her hand and silently waiting to be called on, Alyah sat completely still, smiling and patient. "Good morning Mr. Leroy," called out Alyah. "I was just wondering if you were aware of our ice-cream social that is taking place this month and if you and your wonderful family will be joining us."

Mr. Leroy wasn't completely unaware of the annual dance and ice-cream social, which had been the best part of the year for most of the kids in the past. But he hadn't given much thought to bringing his own daughters and his wife to enjoy the day with his students.

"Good idea Alyah, maybe I will bring my beautiful princesses and my queen to meet all of you and to have some ice-cream," replied Mr. Leroy. Okay, let's get started on learning about poetry."

So, for the next twenty-minutes, Mr. Leroy followed his lesson plan describing what a poem is, why the kids needed to know how to identify a poem along with how some people use poems to share sweet thoughts with one another. He ended by saying that poetry is usually different from writing letters like the kids had been practicing last week.

"Oh yeah, let's learn how to write poems so Crunchy can write his girlfriend Alyah a l-o-v-e poem," called out Jamal.

Jamal had been hard on Crunchy all year, but nothing irritated Crunchy more than when Jamal made fun of how much he thought the world of Alyah.

As the class giggled and almost got out of control, Mr. Leroy calmed them down before the warm fuzzy feeling that Crunchy began to feel turned into a heated spurt of anger towards Jamal.

Crunchy did have nice friends in class who managed to help him deal with his anger.

"Don't worry about Jamal," whispered one of Crunchy's classmates.

The class had known for a while now that Crunchy actual did admire Alyah and that he would love it if she would be his friend.

"Yeah, Crunchy...but you better learn how to spell before giving her your poem, or else she'll be laughing at you too," whispered another classmate.

That morning in class, Crunchy couldn't manage to follow along with any of the lesson. Stanzas. Lines. Rhyme. Meter.

Stanzas...Lines...Rhyme...Meter. None of it made any sense to Crunchy as he kept his head down, hoping that Mr. Leroy avoided calling on him to repeat any of the definitions of the new vocabulary words.

As the class prepared to go home that day, Crunchy couldn't help but to remember when he was a little kid. He thought back to when he was about three or four years old and how Grandad

Noah used to read poems and sing songs to him at their house.

As Crunchy packed up his bag and headed for the door he thought to himself, "If only my grandad was still alive. Maybe he could have been teaching me all I need to know about writing poems?"

The next few days at school were rough for all of the kids in room 227. Whenever there was a new lesson being taught or whenever students were required to think a little harder than the day before, the frustration could be felt a mile away. Most of time, Mr. Leroy's students improved on their skills and achieved the classroom goals. But as the class got closer to the end of the year State Tests, things seemed to get a bit harder. And for Crunchy, who had experienced little success all year, he was now completely in over his head.

Every time Crunchy was confused or frustrated in class he managed to scream out loud which disrupted everyone in the room. When Crunchy was upset with challenging schoolwork he sucked his teeth and grunted, preventing everyone from being able to concentrate. Although his outbursts were causing the class to miss out on learning, his anger also caused him to throw pencils across the room which was even worse than yelling.

One day after class, Mr. Leroy approached Crunchy just before he and his sisters made their way to the front of the school to make their afternoon journey home.

"Hey, Charles...can I talk to you for a minute?" called out Mr. Leroy.

After Mr. Leroy complimented Crunchy by calling him the toughest cookie that he knew on live TV, Crunchy had thought that Mr. Leroy actually believed in him. But as the year got closer and closer to state testing and closer to another inevitable month of summer school, Crunchy didn't know what to believe in anymore.

"Mr. Leroy, don't even worry about it. I know I'm in trouble and I know I'm gonna stay back in the 5th grade. Just...just--"

But before Crunchy could finish his sentence, Mr. Leroy stopped him.

"I wanted to give you a special poem to read and an assignment that is just right for you. This is the poem that I read when I was your age, and it helped me become a great poet, a better reader, and more importantly, it helped me become a better person. Read it to your sisters when you get home and write your own poem that is similar to this one."

An assignment like this should have been easy to complete. The class had been reading poetry and writing their own poems for almost a whole week.

Later on that evening, after Crunchy and his sisters ate dinner, he tried reading the poem to them. But there was one major problem. The poem contained words that he couldn't pronounce and some that he didn't understand. There was also punctuation in the poem that made it difficult to read. And as much as Crunchy wanted the poem to help him the same way that it helped Mr. Leroy, it didn't.

Before bed that night, Crunchy said a prayer that he hoped would be answered to help him become a better reader and what would give him the skills to write his own amazing poem.

The following day at school, the list for the kids who had earned enough scholar dollar points to attend the dance and ice cream social that

Alyah reminded Mr. Leroy about was up on the walls in the hallway.

"Yo...yo...yo...boom. There goes my name," shouted Jamal as he and Kelvin gave each other their special handshake before making their way to class.

"Man, this dance is gonna be the best one ever. And the ice cream...I'm gonna get extra scoops," said Kelvin.

The boys couldn't help but think about being able to hang out with their class, eat ice cream together, and, more importantly, dance and party with the girls! Everyone had been talking about how they were going to be having so much fun, running around, eating ice cream, and doing all of the latest dances.

Every year, Alyah's mother volunteered at events like these to make sure all of the kids were having fun. But the real reason why she had volunteered for the last two years was to make sure no one tried hanging around too close to her daughter.

The news spread quickly about who had earned enough positive behavior and classwork completion points to make it to the event. Back in February, Crunchy had worked extremely hard on his Black History assignment. And although he had done a great job in school for a few days in March and for a couple days in April, unfortunately his frustration, anger, and poor attitude placed him in yet another crunchy situation.

CHAPTER FIVE

On the day of the big school event, Crunchy was preparing himself to miss out on another awesome experience.

Crunchy's scholar dollar points were only one classroom assignment away from him earning his chance to attend the dance. Earlier in the week, Mr. Leroy had provided Crunchy with an extra credit assignment that was supposed to help him by increasing his grade for him to participate in all of the fun.

Before heading to the cafeteria for lunch on the day of the party, Crunchy decided to approach Mr. Leroy with the unfinished poem assignment. Crunchy had tried so hard to understand it but he just couldn't figure out. But there was a reason why the rules in class also included that students should remain in their seats until they are given permission to get up and move around the classroom.

Unaware that Crunchy was walking over to him, Mr. Leroy turned his six-foot four-inch body around in a sudden twist as if he had heard a gigantic linebacker creeping up behind him, ready to tackle him and slam him to the ground. Mr. Leroy's professional football reflexes were being used at the wrong time!

As Crunchy went to tap Mr. Leroy on the shoulder, slam! Mr. Leroy turned his body too fast, knocking into Crunchy, causing Crunchy's feet to leave from underneath him. Crunchy's body hit the ground with a loud thud. At that moment, everyone was completely silent.

When Crunchy woke up, he was sitting on the ground of what seemed to be his classroom in room 227. The desks were arranged in the same order, the posters were all in the same spot, but as he looked up and continued to scan the room, he noticed that something was off. Nobody was in the room with him. Just moments ago, the classroom was full of kids who were eager and excited in anticipation of the music that the DJ at the school dance would play.

But after being knocked down, Crunchy looked around the room, and he didn't see anyone. Crunchy noticed that the bulletin board, which was cleared off before he fell, was now full and redecorated.

Each student had their poem neatly placed on the bulletin board. The latest assignment that they were working on in class was now hanging up in the room. How could this be, he thought? Just a minute ago, there was nothing there!

In the exact center of the bulletin board was a blank spot where it appeared, an entire poem could fit.

Crunchy, sad, and confused began to think about whether or not his class was at the dance without him. Was he too late? Did Mr. Leroy accidentally knock him over, leave him on the ground, and take the class to the gym for the party without him?

"If only I knew how to write a stupid poem, this dumb, corny poem," screamed Crunchy.

Without realizing it, Crunchy had started sobbing and sat back down on the ground. Without warning, a young man in a brand new, all-white tuxedo knocked on the classroom door, startling Crunchy.

"Hey, Hey...what's up," called out the man at the door wearing the most amazing outfit Crunchy had ever seen.

Drying his tears and wiping the snot from his nose, Crunchy responded politely. "Hello, are you a parent chaperoning the dance, where is everybody?" asked Crunchy.

But the man didn't seem to hear what Crunchy had just asked. Instead, he walked over to the bulletin board and pointed to the blank spot. "See here...this is where your poem is supposed to go, Crunchy. We have to get you to write yours so that you can earn your points and make it to the dance," called out the man.

"How do you know about my assignment," asked Crunchy.

"Let's just say I know a lot about a lot of things," replied the man.

For the next several minutes, the man went over the vocabulary words with Crunchy. Stanza. Lines. Rhyme. Meter. Stanza. Lines. Rhyme. Meter. And before he knew it, Crunchy knew that a stanza was the section of the poem and that lines made up the stanza and that sometimes the lines had words that rhyme and that poem could even have a rhythm like a song which was called meter.

After a couple more pointers from the man, Crunchy began to smile and feel confident, not only about the definitions for the parts of a poem but in his ability to write one of his own!

Crunchy took one more stare at the blank space on the bulletin board and imagined that one of his very own poems could be placed right in the center of the board, for everyone to see and for the kids to know that he was good at something.

"Here goes nothing," thought Crunchy.

When I lost my grandad
I lost my best friend
He really loved his family
Now he's blowing in the wind

If only he could see
How strong I try to be
But at night when stars come out
It's hard for me to sleep

My friends are loud and mean
But one is very cool
I wish she knew how much she means
To me when I'm at school

I won't give up at trying hard
And here's the reason why
Someday I'll make my grandad proud
But one piece at a time.

As Crunchy finished writing his poem, the man asked him to read it out loud to him. As Crunchy read the poem, the man smiled from ear to ear. Just as Crunchy went to look up to see the man's reaction to the last line, "*But one piece at a time,*" the man was gone.

Crunchy looked to his left, to his right, and behind him with a perplexed look on his face. There was no sign of the man, anywhere.

CHAPTER SIX

"Charles, Charles, wake up...are you okay," shouted Mr. Leroy.

Crunchy had been knocked out cold. He was on the ground, still holding his assignment in his hand.

Crunchy wanted nothing more than to prove that he had learned enough about poetry so that Mr. Leroy would allow him to participate in the dance. But approaching Mr. Leroy without making sure Mr. Leroy saw him coming backfired on Crunchy.

Closing his eyes and over exaggerating, Kelvin called out while pretending to faint as Jamal held him up. "Crunchy, don't die on me, Crunchy...wake up Crunchy". The kids couldn't help but laugh at Kelvin, as they realized that Crunchy was going to be okay.

"Crunchy...oh lord, Crunchy was a good man," continued Kelvin pretending that he was delivering a speech at Crunchy's funeral.

As the boys begin to show their true feelings for Crunchy, joking or not, in what was just a moment of panic, Crunchy rolled over with a deep breath and a fresh wave of energy as he shot up like a rocket to his feet.

"Mr. Leroy, I was trying to talk to you about poetry before you made the final decision about the dance. I know it was hard for me, and I don't think I understand it all yet, but don't give up on me. I'm gonna get better at reading, but I know that I'll do it one piece at a time."

Mr. Leroy and the rest of the class was unprepared for what they were getting ready to hear. "Well, Charles...what's in your hand," asked Mr. Leroy. "Now that you are okay, how about you tell me how I can help you, and maybe we can work something out so that you can enjoy the dance," suggested Mr. Leroy.

Crunchy looked down in his hand at what he was sure would be his half-finished poem from the night before. His original assignment that he tried to create failed to include stanzas, lines, rhyme, and meter. But instead, when Crunchy brought the paper to his face, there in his hand was a completed poem with four stanzas and a beautiful title, "Grandad's Timing."

Crunchy couldn't believe what he was seeing. It was the poem that the man had helped him make just before Mr. Leroy and the class woke him up from being knocked out.

The look on Crunchy's face gave off the impression that something was wrong. As Crunchy began reading the poem out loud to Mr. Leroy, he did so without noticing that the entire class was now tuned in and quietly listening to him.

**(Whole class gathering around
and respectfully listening)**

Grandad's Timing, by Crunchy Thomas

"When I lost my grandad
I lost my best friend
He really loved his family
Now he's blowing in the wind

If only he could see
How strong I try to be
But at night when stars come out
It's hard for me to sleep

My friends are loud and mean
But one is very cool
I wish she knew how much she means
To me when I'm at school

I won't give up at trying hard
And here's the reason why
Someday I'll make my grandad proud
But one piece at a time."

Mr. Leroy couldn't believe what he had just heard. The entire class stood in awe of Crunchy's amazing, heartfelt poem. It was breathtaking. It was beautiful. It was perfect. "Crunchy, Mr. Leroy knocked some sense into you, bruh," jokingly added Jamal.

And with that being said, Mr. Leroy looked over at an empty bulletin board. And as he walked towards it, he did so while saying that he had the perfect spot in the room for such a fantastic poem. Mr. Leroy took the finished poem out of Crunchy's hands, placed it in a special paper protecting sleeve, and stapled it to the wall.

"Well...I'm sure you know what this means, Crunchy," called out Mr. Leroy.

Crunchy was going to the dance! He had completed an assignment that showed Mr. Leroy how much he had been paying attention. It was clear to Mr. Leroy how hard Crunchy had been trying to put the pieces of his life together.

As the kids all ran around in the gymnasium, listening to their favorite songs, doing their favorite dances, and eating their favorite ice cream, Alyah had made her way over to where Crunchy was hanging out.

"Hello there, Charles. I hope you are enjoying our celebration. We have worked really hard this year preparing for the sixth-grade," said Alyah.

Crunchy was shocked. This was the first time all year that Alyah had even said his name! Not only was she talking to him but she was "hoping that he was enjoying the celebration".

His words were trapped somewhere behind the large bite of freezing cold ice-cream that he plopped in his mouth just seconds before Alyah walked over and spoke to him.

"Oh Yup, I am," nervously stumbled Crunchy.

He had been waiting all year to talk to his crush, and all he could think of was a brilliant four-word phrase.

"And by the way, your grandad would be really proud of you," added Alyah.

At that point, Crunchy had heard enough from Alyah to be satisfied for the rest of his life. She had made his entire day. In fact, she had made his week. As a matter of fact, she had probably made his whole year!

As the dance and ice-cream social came to a close, the kids in room 227 would head home that day with a sense of love and joy in their hearts as they were all proud of Crunchy for not giving up on his school work and for doing something that they all knew would have made his grandad smile.

As Crunchy headed downstairs to pick up his sisters from the auditorium so that the three of them could make their way home, Crunchy began to brag about how well he did on writing his poem. But before he could get out a complete sentence, he decided instead to remind himself once more that improvement in school was possible but that it would happen by putting his past mistakes behind him and learning to forgive and let go of heartache and pain, not by bragging.

CHAPTER SEVEN

The month of May was finally here. And for the third, fourth, and fifth-graders at Elite Public Charter School in Washington, D.C, it meant that the big state tests were officially only days away.

Usually, when the weather warms up, kids all around the country gain a sense of excitement in hopes of hitting the pools after Memorial Day.

But instead, being this close to the big tests

caused the students in Mr. Leroy's class to become overwhelmed with anxiety and fear. So to them, the month of May meant that for six whole days, they would have to focus like they've never focused before.

The teachers had tried their hardest all year to prepare students for success. And now, all the kids could do was try their best. A small select group of students knew that scoring low on the big state tests meant attending summer school. The big state tests always had a way of ruining summer plans for a family or two.

Most of the kids in room 227 had known for a few weeks now that they had learned enough and had proven to enough people that the sixth-grade is where they would be next school year.

For students like Charles Anthony Thomas, aka Crunchy, who learned a little different than the other kids, it meant that there would be an end of the year meeting coming up. The meeting would be held to discuss his behavior. Rating how Crunchy behaved during the school year, along with adding up his test scores, would be how the staff at EPCS would determine if Crunchy was sixth-grade material.

Those big scary meetings only took place for certain students. And Crunchy's special end of the year meeting would be attended by everyone; the school counselor Mrs. Moniz, the school Principal Mrs. Morris, his classroom teacher Mr. Leroy as well as his mother and his grandma, Ms. Jones and Grandma Clara.

Although testing and school was a significant part of Crunchy's life, it wasn't the only thing on his mind.

For kids like Charles and his sisters, who grow up without a father or a positive male role model, certain events like birthdays or holidays can be challenging to deal with. Seeing the other kids in the neighborhood receive presents or gifts throughout the year was tough, especially considering that Crunchy's mom and grandma were barely keeping food on the table for a group of fast-growing kids.

But there was one particular occasion that Crunchy and his two sisters eagerly looked forward to celebrating every year.

As the fifth-grade students in room 227 were preparing one last time before taking the first of their end of the year state test, they couldn't ignore the fact that Mother's Day was just around the corner. Even though Crunchy's mother and grandma had plenty to be thankful for, like good health and the roof over their heads, as Crunchy got older, he began to notice that the special women in his life seemed to get sad around Mother's Day.

So as the weekend got closer, Crunchy had an idea. He wanted to cheer up everyone in his house. But Crunchy wasn't quite sure if the sadness that his mother and grandma experienced during these special occasions was from how much everyone missed Grandad Jones. He was determined to make a difference in everyone's mood.

The Friday before the Mother's Day weekend had flown by.

"Good afternoon, class," called out Mr. Leroy.

Mr. Leroy had been putting in extra hours at work as he began to get the hang of teaching. Not only had he been preparing his students for successful days of testing on the big State Tests, but he was also beginning to feel more comfortable in his role as an educator. One thing that Mr. Leroy did that not many teachers before had done for the kids at EPCS was interview them. One by one, he found time to sit them down, ask them relevant questions, and found out what some of the most challenging things were for the kids.

His interview with Kelvin was really helpful. He had asked Kelvin a bunch of things.

Kelvin's responses: "*So...sometimes, I'm loud when I'm not supposed to be. My teachers have told my mother every time they see her that I have so much potential, but I already know that. I usually get in trouble for talking and being out of my seat and not because I want to get in trouble, but because being in our school is too exciting to stay in one spot all day. I kind of don't understand why we always get in trouble for standing up, but like, I know that they want us to listen and not get in trouble, so I try my hardest to follow the rules. One thing that I still don't understand is why the school has those crazy behavior rules or like, behavior policy things. And recess is short. And the food-- The food is mainly nasty, and sometimes I get so hungry by 1:30 that it don't even matter and I eat it anyway. I also disagree with the time we have specials because it's right in the morning, and then we have to sit down and learn for the whole rest of the day. I hate going to art, P.E, music and Spanish class in the mornings and then not having another fun class until the next day. And also the after-care program doesn't have sports for us and they should because the boys in aftercare are very active and like to play football, basketball and other types of sports, but they don't have that."*

Mr. Leroy took the information from all of us, and he did stuff about it. He lets us stand up when we are working, he brings extra tasty snacks for when we are starving, and he lets us play vocabulary games that feel like gym class. As the year moves along, Mr. Leroy just keeps getting better and better as a teacher.

I can't believe that its already May. This meant that the big state test was getting closer. The class was also sure that Mr. Leroy was going to plan something else really cool and special for the class.

"Alright...as most of you know, we are getting ready for the end of the year assessments, but I don't want anyone to lose track of how special this weekend ahead of us is," exclaimed Mr. Leroy.

For the last several weeks, Crunchy had known that his mother, grandma, and aunt, who often stayed the night over Crunchy's grandma's house with her kids, were saving up to host a huge Mother's Day dinner for all of the moms in the Jones Family.

"Is anyone doing anything super special on Sunday," asked Mr. Leroy.

As the kids gazed around the room on that Friday afternoon, they seemed nervous to speak. No one seemed willing to share how excited they were to honor their mothers and grandmas. It was as if speaking up and opening up about loving the adults in their lives would tarnish their *tough kid* reputations. The room lay awkwardly silent.

A student that Mr. Leroy hadn't really heard much from all year was sitting with her face down, tilted at a 45-degree angle, the *fake reading* angle that most of the kids in room 227 had mastered over the years to avoid being called on. Kymora, the quiet, shy, but brilliant student in the class seemed to be melting in her seat, as if hoping to become instantly invisible.

"Kymora...are you and your family doing anything special for your mother," asked Mr. Leroy.

As Kymora slowly lifted up her head, it was clear at that point that tears were swelling up in her eyes. The kids had known that Kymora's mother wasn't the *best mom* in town ever since the 2nd grade when she came to school, shouting and yelling about how she wished she never gave birth to any kids. Kymora was the youngest of five and had four older brothers. Her older brothers were guys who got into way more trouble than just your every day "crunchy situation".

Kymora's older brothers were the guys in the neighborhood who gave her family a bad reputation. Two of her brothers were now teenagers and were both caught selling drugs and fighting, a bunch of times. So we kind of felt bad for Kymora because she was a really nice friend of ours. But her brothers, they drove her mom crazy and made her mom feel like they were all a mistake, including Kymora.

"Mr. Leroy...I don't really do nothing for mother's day," sighed Kymora.

"Being the only girl in my house is like being alone all of the time because all I can do is wait for my cousins to come over, and if they don't, my mom makes me stay away from my brothers. I usually have no one to talk to. And sometimes, my aunt is there to hang out with me, but she usually only comes over when my brothers are fighting with my mom. They stay up really late, and they tell me that school is for losers. They play their music really loud, and they smoke and do bad things. I can't ever really sleep."

"Kymora...thank you for sharing, and I am sorry that your brothers don't see how important it is to be better role models for you," replied Mr. Leroy.

"My mom also tells me that school isn't important, and she doesn't seem to care as much as you do about me, and that's crazy to me because I don't even know you like I know my mother," said Kymora.

"Well...maybe this time, you can make a card for your mom and share with her how you feel. Maybe you can be the person who shows her how important it is to love one another and why being a close family is so important. I will make sure to pray for you, your brothers and your mother over the weekend," said Mr. Leroy with a warm smile on his face.

"How about you, Charles. Anything special happening this weekend for the hard-working women who take care of you and your sisters," asked Mr. Leroy.

Crunchy hesitated. He wanted to explain that his mother, grandma, and aunt were planning on cooking all night to have the biggest feast that they've ever hosted for the family. But something deep inside of Crunchy held onto sharing the news. Instead, Crunchy played along with the crowd of kids and shrugged his shoulders.

"Alright, well, I'll be taking my family out to a wonderful Sunday evening dinner to celebrate how much my daughters and I appreciate my wife and her mother. On behalf of the Leroy family, be sure to tell all of your mothers happy--"

But before Mr. Leroy could finish his thought, the kids all looked up at the clock, and like Olympic sprinters, they charged out of the room, ignoring Mr. Leroy's final message and headed out to the front of the school for dismissal.

What was happening in room 227 that was so important to the 5th graders at EPCS? Was it something that Mr. Leroy said that caused them all to run out of the room as if the building was on fire? Based on how the day ended, Mr. Leroy began second-guessing his efforts as a teacher. Had everything he'd done all year just fly out of the window. He was at a lost for words. He was now worried more than ever about if he was actually making an impact on his students' lives. Mr. Leroy was convinced that his students were still far away from being prepared for middle school.

Special words from the author

Windows of opportunity

When you are unsure about the direction your life is taking, **examine** your situation a little closer. When you are confused about something, the world can seem like a much larger and complicated place. By failing to learn and apply the life-changing lessons that your experiences have the power in teaching you, growing is difficult. Making the most out of life isn't an easy or comfortable process. But these experiences should make you more curios instead of causing you to stop trying or **persisting**.

I would argue that the majority of people in our world deal with the ups and downs of emotionally readjusting their outlook on life.

Sometimes, the help you need to get on track or back on the path to a successful future doesn't come in the obvious package marked, "The Guide to Figuring Out Your Life". But in some cases, it does.

Take, for instance, someone who wakes up in their home one morning, and to their surprise, smoke has filled their entire house. Immediately, this person would assume that they are in some type of danger. How much danger and how much panic they should exhibit are relative to the person's preparation for such an emergency.

Once it becomes clear that A, they have time to figure out the source of the smoke, and B, they more than likely will be able to save their home from burning to the ground, the person then has choices to make. But now, for instance, let's assume the worst within this unwanted scenario. Instead of having time to figure out how serious of an issue this smoke has caused, let us pretend that this person wakes up to a fire that is blazing and growing at a rapid rate.

In this case, the individual would absolutely be at a panic, to find themselves in need of the most immediate and effective support. So, to their rescue comes a helicopter. Not just any helicopter but one that is specifically used to rescue individuals and families from scenarios like this one, from a burning home.

What does the person do next? They get to the window and reach out to the stationary ladder, that's pressed firmly against the side of the house. With the proper and necessary equipment, a rescue worker meets the man or woman who is in dire need of an emergency evacuation, wraps the harness around them and subsequently lifts them off to safety.

In this case, the person who was just rescued

will have a second chance at life. And after the damages are repaired and the home is either replaced or rebuilt, the individual who was saved will have an opportunity to not only get their life back together, but they will also have a much greater appreciation for what it means to live.

Now assume for a second that once awaken by that blazing fire and moments before choosing to reach out of that window to be saved, that instead, the individual denies the assistance of the emergency helicopter unit, closes the window and accepts the fate of crumbling down in a blaze of smoke and fire with their home and their worldly possessions.

Does this sound crazy? To deny the obvious, lifesaving help of the rescue unit? Well, when people deny reaching for windows of opportunity that can restore their dreams and allow them to be successful in life by finding hope in their goals and aspirations, those same people might as well close that window, inhale the smoke and give up on maximizing their potential in life.

When that individual in the burning house woke up that morning, and they heard and saw the help being offered by the rescue unit, they knew that it wasn't too late to make it out alive and to see another beautiful day.

RESHAPING SUCCESS

Success does not happen for anyone without first experiencing frustration or doubt. To become successful, it takes time. When you first try to accomplish anything in life, if it is meaningful and important to you, there is a huge chance that you will find failure or frustration with it the very first time. That is where being able to **integrate** the failed attempts with new ideas that we get from other experiences comes in handy.

I think it is safe to assume that we have all experienced several examples that fit this suggested experience. Thinking back to the first time I tried making pancakes, I immediately remember how difficult and disastrous this morning had been. Sure, many people can read the directions and assume that they have measured the ingredients accurately enough to successfully feed themselves and those waiting for you to finish cooking.

But like anything in life that you try for the first time, just like those sloppy, burnt, watery pancakes, the failed attempt allowed me to learn how to improve the process for the next time. Through what many refer to as trial and error, I was able to correct the mistakes, by turning the heat down, accurately mixing the appropriate amount of mix and water to not only make some delicious pancakes, but to prove to myself that success comes to those who aren't afraid to fail. Had I scratched the idea of trying to cook pancakes, I would have a limited mindset in regards to finding the success out of failure.

The success is buried, hidden underneath the second or third time you try to do the same task or accomplish the same goal. When you don't give up and find the courage to keep digging and give it your all one final time, the window of opportunity reappears, allowing success to happen as you **construct** your vision for achieving goals right before your eyes.

In school, success can look like getting really good grades on a test or being named Class President. To some, success is when you are able to even make it to school on time. Finishing your coursework and getting an A on a final exam are two different examples of being successful. And the best part about these potential goals is that accomplishing either of them simply takes readjusting your outlook on what you believe you can achieve. If someone has told you it is too late to have success in this capacity, don't waste your time on proving them wrong, but instead, prove yourself right.

So, being a successful person looks completely different depending on the specific time of day, where you are, or what it is that you are doing at that moment in life.

When you find moments where you are successful, it is very important that you allow these experiences to build **confidence** in you as a person. **Confidence** is that feeling you have when you aren't afraid to be the one to take the last shot in the big game. **Confidence** is the feeling you get when it's time to accomplish a huge task or achieve a goal, and you step right up to the plate. **Confidence** is inviting those same people over for breakfast who were there the first time you almost burnt the kitchen down making pancakes.

It is also crucial that you never confuse being confident with being "cocky". Being "cocky" means that if you happen to make that winning basket during a huge basketball game or finish that presentation on time for your boss at work, that after doing so, you run over and rub it in the faces of the other players on the court or co-workers in the office.

Being "cocky" means that you don't think you have to practice as hard as everyone and that you don't think anyone could ever help you to become even better. Instead, believe in yourself but be respectful to others when you happen to achieve greatness.

Some people will tell you that success means that you have to be the best at whatever it is that you are doing. Some people will tell you that to become successful when taking advantage of these windows of opportunity that you must win every game you play in.

But what those people would be forgetting to tell you is that if you can approach life from a once defeated perspective and turn around how you view your opportunities, you would be halfway there. By improving at the skill you are practicing while preparing to take on the opportunities, or standing up to a challenge that was once too scary to face, those moments are also preparing you for accomplishing success!

The time when I was figuring out the best way for kids to improve their ability at reshaping what success meant to them, had also been around the same time when I met this one student. I had to rub my eyes because of how much he resembled myself. I jokingly went home after the first day of school that year and told my friends that I knew for a fact that I had yet to have a child but that one kid seemed to resemble my own blood-line more than my known relatives did.

Known as one of the most impulsive and violent students in the building, I immediately knew that I had to find a way to harness his energy. Relationships have been a common theme within my classroom and school community that year. So, naturally, I thought, the more I know about a child and his or her family, the more of a handle I could have on their behaviors and on getting them to maximize their effort to focus and concentrate on a successful school year.

This held some truths throughout the year, but again, building authentic relationships with students who have had difficult and challenging upbringings, finding it hard to trust strangers or the adults known as "teachers" wasn't an easy task to manage.

Take, for instance, this one classroom where a former student of mine was a part of before promoting to the next grade where I became his teacher. The class that this young man had come from a year ago had been so poorly managed and improperly configured that the initial teacher quit after only two weeks of school. The same class, where this young man was a member of would find itself under the reigns of five different teachers in the course of ten months. So, inconsistent adult supervision and random lesson planning, underserved a mission of closing the space that the achievement gap had created, leaving no chance at making any improvement for those thirty-one students the year prior.

For reasons that I didn't understand, I decided to grow my hair out that school year. After about a year of not cutting the top of my hair, it grew into a Mohawk like shape, where keeping the sides groomed and faded turned it into a stylish, hip new look. At the same time, the professional football player Odell Beckham Jr. was performing as an NFL superstar, and coincidently enough, his hairstyle, that mine closely resembled, became a household trend.

I naturally connected with the young men in my classes as a school teacher for several reasons, some more obvious at times than others. However, during this pivotal time in popular culture, the boys in my classroom identified with me because of how similar this superstar athlete and I's hairstyles were. So, on occasion, I would see the boys coming in weekend after weekend with their hair a little longer on the top and twisted as they were preoccupied with twirling their fingers in their hair almost as if to stretch it and style it like Odell Beckham Jr's or...mine.

Behavior trackers where you know...teachers check in with kids who aren't doing that great weren't working for this young man in the beginning of the year. So almost in desperation, I offered to cut his hair and style it like mine if he could record one day without being aggressive and disruptive in class.

After he managed to behave ideally for one day, he came to me the very next day and asked me when I was going to cut it. To keep my promise, I asked him if he thought one day of behaving was easy to do. Eventually, I convinced him that if he could behave appropriately and complete most of his work for one whole month, that I would cut his hair and "hook him up".

Needless to say, I have cut his hair four times this year, extending the amount of time he had to perform to the best of his ability, along with behaving appropriately. His success was reshaped by a very non-traditional way, but it worked for him. During his yearly meeting with all of his teachers, or principal and his mom, where we all met twice a year to update his learning goals, his mother couldn't hold back her tears and we read his data report on the growth that he made that no one said was possible as a reading and math student.

More importantly, to mention, he went from being sent out one hundred and seven times last year to being sent out ten times in the entire year, less than twelve months ago. This was perhaps the miracle that happens once in an entire teaching career, and I was fortunate enough to be a part of it for him.

When I asked him how he felt about school, he said to me that, "You were kind of like a father to me and not having a father at all, having one at school was...ugh…it was cool man. I felt great this year because I used to be off-task and get into a lot of trouble, but I did a lot better this year. And I didn't get in a lot of suspensions like I did last year. I didn't know how to be successful, and I didn't know what being successful looked like until now".

If you learned anything from this example, it might be that success is what you make it. It comes in even more ways than decreasing the number of negative phone calls home you receive or when you lower the number of times you're kicked out of class. Surprisingly, success can even come in the form of how often you treat others the way you would like to be treated.

ABOUT THE AUTHOR

Glen Leroy Mourning was born on March 26th, 1987, in Danbury, Connecticut. As the oldest of his mother Lillian's five children, Glen was blessed with the opportunity to lead by example where he would become the first of two generations to not only graduate from high school but to complete a master's degree.

In 2005 Glen earned a Full- Athletic Scholarship to attend the University of Connecticut, where he would make the All-Big East Conference Academic Honor roll for two years in a row before graduating and attending Grad School at the University of Bridgeport.

In 2010 Glen finished his master's degree in Elementary Ed. and was named the student-teacher of the year at the University of Bridgeport. Since then, Glen worked alongside the nationally renowned Educational contributor Dr. Steve Perry, Star of the CNN Special "Black in America II" and the host of TV One's "Save our Sons."

As a 4th and 5th grade teacher at Capital Preparatory Magnet School in Hartford, Connecticut, Glen managed to brilliantly inspire the lives of hundreds of students in his tenure as an educator. At the same time, he was the assistant varsity football coach at Capital Prep, where the team posted an incredible record of 22-2, winning State playoff appearances before stepping down from his role as the defensive backs coach.

For the past few year, Glen has worked in Washington D.C area as a 5th grade teacher. Glen and his wife Nicole will continue working together in education where they hope to continue writing and sharing literature for young people in America.

Glen's greatest accomplishments are not those that have occurred on the playing fields across America but rather with his promise to his family that he has kept, which was to become the motivation for his students that have come from similar circumstances.

More from the Author

Crunchy Life Book 1: Recess Detention

In book 1 of the Crunchy Life Series, students are challenged to think about what challenges they face daily that may distract them from being the best that they can be. Students often face problems that can easily overwhelm them, but what may also be hard for a kid to communicate to adults. Keep track of how Crunchy attempts to make smart choices in a confusing and challenging world. When times are tough, be sure to find positive people to surround yourself with.

Crunchy Life Book 2: Naughty of Nice

In book 2 of the Crunchy Life Series, students are challenged to think about times where they have had to serve a consequence after making a poor choice. Students often struggle with feeling as if they are bad kids. But in reality, sometimes kids simply make "bad" choices. Keep track of how Crunchy responds to his challenges. Always make good choices to avoid being naughty.

Crunchy Life Book 3: Tough Cookies

In book 3 of the Crunchy Life Series, students are challenged to have an open mind and hear from multiple perspectives. Students often struggle with learning new information, especially if it goes against what adults tell them. Keep track of how Crunchy grows as a thinker, as well as how he builds his confidence. Always be willing to learn new things!

Crunchy Life Book 5: Every Point Counts

In book 5 of the Crunchy Life Series, students are challenged to be honest with themselves about whether or not they give 100 percent in the things that they set out to accomplish. Students often feel as though they are trying their best, especially on the things that they care about. However, with a little self-reflecting, students can find ways to dig deeper to improve their lives even more. Keep track of how Crunchy realizes that he has more in him on his way to success. Always give life your best shot.

Care More Than Us: The Young People's Guide to Success and student work book.

"Care More Than Us" is a conversation style read for young readers and teenagers alike, who may have trouble identifying how great they or their students and children already are. By readjusting what it means to be successful, "Care More Than Us" takes the readers through the process of learning to believe in themselves and avoiding the crowd that may distract them from reaching their goals.

For more information, visit www.glenmourning.com.

Made in the USA
Middletown, DE
04 December 2022

15809102R00064